Book #1

SECRET AGENT MJJ
The Missing Princess

Marc John Jefferies

Big Smile Inc.

New York • Philadelphia • Los Angeles

CH

Book #1

SECRET AGENT MJJ
The Missing Princess
Marc John Jefferies

Written by: Danny Hirsch and S.A. Katz
Cover Illustration by: Doina Paraschiv

Produced by:
Marc A. Jefferies, Big Smile, Inc.

No part of this publication may be produced in whole or in part, or stored in a retrieval system, or transmitted in any form or by any means, electronic, mechanical, photocopying, recording, or otherwise, without written permission, write to:
Big Smile, Inc., Attention: Marc A. Jefferies
117 Cherry Valley Point, Stroudsburg, Pennsylvania 18360
or email: marcjohnjefferies@yahoo.com

ISBN # 0-9761891-0-0
LCCN # 2005900629

The Missing Princess
Written by: Danny Hirsch and S.A. Katz
Cover Illustration & Book Design: Doina Paraschiv

Printed in the U.S.A.
First printing January 2005

CONTENTS

A Letter To My Readers

A LETTER TO MY READERS

Dear Friends,

Thanks for reading the first book in the Secret Agent MJJ series: The Missing Princess. I hope that you like it. To make certain that you enjoy it the best that you can, I've provided a Director's Sheet to help explain words that may be unfamiliar to you and a Gyroscope that explains some of the real people and places in the story. Both of these can be found in the back of this book and as always, if you need more information, check out a dictionary or your local library. Who knows? Maybe there you'll stumble onto your own adventures. Until then, read, enjoy, be kind to others and hang on tight because this ride is about to begin.

As Always,
-MJJ, The Real Deal

ACT 1:
WELCOME TO WEIRD

What you are about to read may surprise you. It still surprises me, even after all that I have been through.

My name is Marc John Jefferies. Many of you may have seen me on TV or in a few movies. I'm an actor, and at thirteen I would say a pretty good one, not because of the roles that I have starred in, but because of the secret that I guard everyday. It is a secret that not even my family knows about. It is a secret that keeps the world safe and I am here to share it with you. You all know who I am in public. Now I will tell you the whole story, a story about the other me: Marc John Jefferies, the secret agent known as Boogieman.

* * *

It all started last year. I was shooting a movie on location on an island in the South Pacific. This place was spectacular. The sun was bright. There was a little breeze but the water was warm and all I wanted to do was hangout on the beach. What kid wouldn't? I'm just like most kids my age, not too tall, but definitely not too short. I have dark brown hair and light brown eyes. I love sports, especially Yankees' baseball. And of course, I really love to watch movies and play video games. Like I said, I'm a pretty normal kid, so while I do everything else, there is always a good bit of homework to complete. Homework's a drag, because as an actor I get to travel all over the world. I've been just about everywhere and let me tell you what kind of strange things I've seen!

But the life of an actor is not always glam and glitz. There is work that needs to be done and I knew that the sand and surf would have to wait. Besides that, my big scene with the famous star Ralph Gibson was about to take place and I would not have missed it for the world!

I took my position on the set where the first scene of the movie would take place. Ralph greeted me with a smile and shook my hand.

"Gooday' mate," Ralph said with a wink.

'Nice guy,' I thought to myself. I hope that you all get to meet him one day.

"Places," called one of the crew members.

"Rolling," said another.

"And, action!" shouted Glen.

2

I was just about to speak my first line when...

"Chirp, chirp, chirp."

It sounded like a funky electronic bird singing somewhere.

"Chirp, chirp, chirp."

Glen yelled...

"Cut!"

Glen turned and walked a short distance from where we stood. We all stopped what we were doing and waited for instructions. I thought nothing of it. Most likely there was a problem with the sound or something else. This was normal. Someone probably just cued the wrong background noise. We would be going at it again in no time. At least that is what I thought until Glen approached me. His face was very serious.

"What was that chirping?" I asked him.

Glen looked around and pulled the tiniest cell phone that I have ever seen from his shirt pocket.

"It was this," he whispered.

"Glen, why are you whispering?" I asked in a low voice.

"Shh," he said in a whisper. He looked to his left. He looked to his right. "Marc, I think that you better take this phone call."

He handed me the small phone and kept peering about anxiously. I was just about to put the phone to my ear when he stopped me.

"Why don't you go back to your trailer," he whispered again before looking around. "And make sure you're alone."

I'll be the first to admit, Glen is a weird man. He's very skinny with a long face, and he's very nervous and always stressed out. He eats nothing but avocado and Spam sandwiches and insists upon wearing the same baseball cap until he finishes filming a movie. I mean that he wears the hat the entire time! He even swims with it on. Really, I saw him do it once. My dad calls him eccentric. You know what I mean? He's really weird but in a cool way. But this phone call and the whispering...this was truly strange, even for Glen.

"Don't let anyone see," he whispered again looking anxiously around us both. "Put that in your pocket until you get where you're going!"

He put his hand over his eyes.

"Hurry," he said and shooed me away toward my trailer with his hand.

I quickly pocketed the phone and made my way to my trailer. Glen was acting a little freaky and my curiosity was getting the better of me. All I could think about was yanking the tiny phone out of my pocket and saying hello. I decided against it. Who knew who or what was on the other end.

After walking by the food line, the microphone guy, the make-up tables and a group of girls who were waiting around for autographs (I stopped to sign a few, I'll admit it), I finally arrived at my trailer. I bounded up the steps, ran inside and swung the door shut behind me.

My trailer was a mess, which is normal. My parents say that I need to keep it clean, but it's a hard thing to do. When we're on location, I do everything there from schoolwork to memorizing lines.

I quickly ran my eyes around the room. No one was there. After making certain that I was alone, I pulled the phone from its hiding place in the cargo pocket of my shorts.

"Hello," I said into the receiver.

A man answered on the other end.

"Marc John Jefferies?" he asked. His voice was gravelly. He sounded very old.

"Yes," I replied. "I'm Marc John Jefferies."

"Thank goodness," said the gravel voiced man. "The world needs you."

"Excuse me?" I replied.

"The world needs you," he said again. "Listen carefully."

How could I not listen carefully? I was just told that the world needed me. How could the world need me? I was only thirteen.

"Do you know who you are, Marc?" asked the man.

"I don't understand," I replied. "What do you

mean?"

"Do you know who you are? Do you know where you came from?"

"Yes," I replied. "From Marc Antonio Jefferies and LaShawn Denise Jefferies, my parents."

The man chuckled slightly. His voice loosened up and no longer sounded as harsh as before.

"Very good," he said, laughing through his words. "Clever boy. But do you know where they came from?"

I was about to answer that they had come from my grandparents, but I had a funny feeling that this was not what he was talking about.

"No, sir," I said. "Tell me."

"Oh, I can't tell you, not on the phone," he answered. His voice was serious once more. "It's too dangerous, Marc. No. You must go somewhere secure, for the information that I am about to share with you has been guarded for centuries."

"Who are you?" I demanded. "What information?"

"Go to Glen," he said. "Tell him that it's okay to come out and play now. That's the secret password. Did you get that? It's okay to come out and play. Say it back to me."

I wasn't sure what was happening. Was this a joke? I decided to play along, just for fun.

"It's okay to come out and play," I said smiling.

"Good," replied the old man. "That's it. Now go and find Glen. He will tell you all that you need to know, Marc."

"How do you know my name?" I asked. "Who is this?"

The man laughed again.

"This is why you have been chosen. Because you, my boy, know all of the right questions to ask. This is why the world needs you," he said. "Patience. Glen has the answers that you need. In the meantime, hide this secret carefully. No one must ever know that we have spoken. It could bring great harm to those around you. Do you understand?"

I still was not sure what the man was asking. But to be safe, I agreed not to talk to anyone else about our conversation until I had a chance to speak in private with Glen.

"I understand," I said.

"Good," he replied. "The world needs you Marc John Jefferies. Now go and find your answers."

There was a click on the other end of the line and the man was gone. I put the phone back in my pocket and set out to find Glen. I needed to know what was happening.

ACT 2:
SECRETS

I didn't need to go far to find Glen. When I opened my door, he was waiting for me right outside. He was standing on a barrel with his face pressed against the glass of one of the trailer windows.

"I have a question for you, Glen," I said.

My voice startled him, and when he jumped, the barrel tipped. Glen fell to the ground with a thump. Aside from being nervous, he was also a clutz.

"Oh boy, oh no, oh boy, oh no," he responded, clutching his elbow. He let go of it as his head slumped over to rest in his hands. "I was afraid you'd have questions for me."

"Oh," I said. "Here's your phone back."

I handed it to him and he snatched it from me, quickly shoving it into his pocket all in one motion. He stood there shaking his head back and forth as he brushed the dirt off of his legs. I asked my first question.

"There was an old guy on the phone who told me that I can 'go out and play' or 'come out and play.' What does that mean?"

"He told you that it was 'okay to come out and play?'" asked Glen.

I nodded my head yes. Glen's face became even more serious than before.

"Oh boy," exclaimed Glen once more. "I was afraid that he told you that."

"Glen, what's going on?"

"Oh boy, oh no, oh boy, then it's all right on schedule and I just forgot." he said.

Suddenly his face perked up. He stood up straight. The wrinkles in his forehead smoothed out. Glen, for the first time since I'd known him, appeared calm and relaxed, almost normal. Almost.

"Come on," he said. "We have important work to do, and it's not this movie."

"What work?" I asked.

"Shhh," he cautioned without turning his head. "We mustn't speak too loudly. The world needs you Marc John Jefferies and we can't take any chances."

"Wait a minute. How did you know that?" I asked. "That's what the man said, and I just got off of the phone a moment ago."

"I've known for years," he said. "Ever since you

and I shot our first movie together. Now come. We've important business to attend to and we can't delay. Walk with me."

"But I have questions," I continued.

We went right back to the set. Glen cupped his hands up around his mouth and made an announcement.

"Lunch!" he shouted to the cast and crew.

I looked down at my watch. It was only 10:30 in the morning. But then again, everyone else on the set knew how weird Glen was. Without a word, they all stopped what they were doing and went to find food. That poor caterer; the last I saw, he hadn't had a chance to put away breakfast yet.

"Come on." Glen motioned me with his hand. "We'll talk in my trailer."

He looked carefully over his shoulder before we made another pass by the food line. It was a huge mess. There were one hundred hungry people pushing and shoving, while the chef, who I must admit was pretty angry with Glen, scrambled to fill plastic bowls with potato salad.

We walked back past where the microphone guy normally stands, past the make-up tables, and past another group of girls who were waiting around for autographs. I didn't stop this time.

Soon, I found myself in Glen's trailer. It was messier than mine. Old tins of Spam were everywhere. Clothes were scattered on the floor. Piles of scripts sat in a corner. Books were stacked on his couch; so many in fact that you could no longer sit on it. He had a small refrigerator at one end and it was covered in dust. But on top of it, heaped neatly in a beautiful glass bowl, were giant avocados. They were bigger than any I'd ever seen and cleaner than anything else in Glen's trailer. The dish that held them was probably the nicest thing in his trailer; the kind of thing that if I broke it at my own house, I'd be in some deep trouble.

"Sit down," he said.

Two plain wooden bar stools stood squarely in the center of his floor. I chose one and waded through the junk-yard of Glen's possessions to get to it. Aside from the avocados, the wooden stools were the only things in the trailer that weren't covered with clutter.

"Now, let's see," said Glen. He looked around the room as if he lost something. "Oh yes," he continued as he walked over to the window.

He reached above his head, grasped the shade in his hand and pulled it down over the window. Then he went around the trailer and did the same with the other shades.

"Glen," I said. "I can't see."

"Don't worry," came Glen's voice from the darkness. "I can take care of that."

A tiny light suddenly clicked on above, illuminating me and the empty stool next to where I sat. Glen suddenly appeared from the darkness and joined me in the small pool of light.

"That just about does it," he said. "Now, let's see."

Again he glanced around the room, looking for something.

"Oh yes," he said.

Glen reached toward his head and after carefully gripping the brim, removed his baseball cap for the first time. Out from underneath fell piles and piles of wavy blond hair. The golden tresses fell in waves down over his face until the entire mane suddenly collapsed onto his shoulders. With all of that hair and his skinny frame he looked more like an underfed lion than a man. I had never seen so much hair! And I wondered if it had ever been cut.

When the last of it had fallen over his face, I saw what appeared to be a small satellite dish sticking out of the top of his head. He reached up toward it, plucked the item from where it sat and set it on the stool next to me.

I could finally make out the whole device. It was indeed a tiny satellite dish attached to a small grey box. A little keyboard stuck out from the side.

"What is that?" I asked.

Glen reached up to his face, pulled some of the

hair away and replaced his cap to hold the over-growth out of his way.

"That, Marc John Jefferies, is a petit operational kit with an electronic yap. But you can just call it a POKEY."

"What does it do?" I asked.

"Everything," he responded.

"What's an electronic yap?" I inquired.

"The electronic yap is my favorite part," he said. His face beamed with excitement. "Listen."

Glen pressed a button and a loud barking noise burst from a speaker on the side of the device.

"That, Marc, is an electronic yap." He seemed pleased with himself as he continued. "Headquarters felt that the contraption wasn't user friendly, so they added the barking sound, the electronic yap to help. Now it feels a lot less like an uncomfortable heavy piece of cold metal and more like a pet. In fact, the electronic yap was my idea. I've grown quite fond of it."

"So that's why you always wear a hat," I said.

"That and my hair," he responded. "My hair always gets in my face."

"You said headquarters. What are you talking about?" I asked. Questions were coming into my head faster than I could ask them.

"We'll get to that in a minute," replied Glen.

"But why not just carry the POKEY in a bag?" I asked.

Glen looked frightened.

"Heavens no, Marc." He was nervous again. "I did that once and almost lost it in the Hippopotamus cage at the zoo. It's amazing how much damage a Hippo can do with a POKEY."

I was just about to ask him about it when he interrupted me. He put both hands out in front of him as a sign for me to slow down.

"But that's a story for another day," he said. "So many questions. Are you ready for the show?"

Glen smiled.

"I guess," I replied.

"Good," he responded. "Because the world needs you, Marc John Jefferies."

Glen suddenly pushed a button on the POKEY and a little lens popped out of its top.

"Lights!" shouted Glen. He clapped his hands twice and we were in darkness.

Suddenly the POKEY projected a blue light onto the window shade in front of us. The silhouette of a man's head moved into the picture. The shadow began to speak.

"Greetings, crime fighter," said the shadow.

I immediately recognized the voice. It was the gravelly old man from the cell phone call.

"Brace yourself," he continued. "For your time has come."

Act 3:
THE ORDER OF THE CAT

I stared at the silhouette projected onto Glen's window shade. There was not much to it: a gray figure on a blue background.

"You're the man from the phone call," I said.

"Yes," replied the silhouette.

"You never told me your name." My curiosity was now getting the best of me. At least, that's how my mom always puts it.

"You're right." The gravel voiced man chuckled slightly. "But you never asked."

"Enough riddles," I said. "What's your name?"

"It depends on who you ask, but most people simply call me Millenia."

"Millenia? That's a strange name," I told the man.

"It's an even stranger story," he said. "But that is for another time. Shall we continue?"

"Yes," I said as I shook my head. I needed to hear

more and fast.

"Do you know your history?" asked Millenia.

"Yes," I replied. "My parents make certain that I study everyday, even when we're on location. I even have to bring a tutor with me." The thought of more homework made me a little sick.

"Good," he replied. "Because we've got a lot of ground to cover."

Millenia paused, took a deep breath, and in his gravelly voice began to tell the story.

"Our tale begins almost two thousand years ago, along the River Nile in ancient Egypt during the reign of Cleopatra. Alexandria, a beautiful and prosperous city had become a great center of learning, for there was built in that place a library like none other. Its massive collection held what was believed to be all of the world's knowledge. The most brilliant students came from around the globe to study there. They learned about math, science, literature and writing. It was a wonderful time and knowledge flourished. But sadly, it was not to last."

Millenia's voice grew quiet, and for a moment he stopped speaking. When he started to talk again, he sounded sad.

"One day, in that splendid city the great Library of Alexandria caught on fire and burned, destroying all of the scrolls that were stored inside. Cleopatra was devastated and wanted to know who had started the fire.

Rumors spread. Some said that it was the Romans who had started the blaze. Others blamed simple thieves. Still, some in Cleopatra's inner circle thought something else. They suspected something sinister at work."

"What?" I asked. The answers could not come fast enough.

"Some suspected that it may even have been the Order of the Snake, an ancient secret organization determined to spread anarchy and chaos wherever they could."

Millenia's voice began to gain in volume. He grew louder and more forceful. Once again I could hear the excitement.

"Cleopatra never did find out who started the fire. No one knows to this day. But what Cleopatra did know was that she needed to do something to protect the world from this kind of harm. So she summoned the best and brightest students in Alexandria, for let us not forget that they were also the best and brightest in the world. These were all young people, mostly your age Marc, but they were brilliant. They knew every word that was in that library. They were the keepers of the world's knowledge and hope. Cleopatra brought them together to both rebuild and protect the new library and carry on that hope for future generations."

"But it was just a library," I said. "Couldn't the Egyptians just go someplace else and buy new scrolls?"

Millenia chuckled again.

"I wish it had been that easy, Marc. In those days, it was very hard to do so. There were no computers. They had to rewrite everything by hand."

"Oh, man," I said. "It's hard enough just to get my homework done on time, even with my laptop. I can't imagine rewriting an entire library."

Millenia laughed some more and then continued.

"Unfortunately, it was never to be. Egypt fell to the Romans, and the group of brilliant people, by order of Cleopatra, fled to the four corners of the earth to hide. Before they did so, she gave them a mission: to fight evil and spread goodness wherever they traveled so that other places would not suffer the same fate. She even gave them a name befitting their position of honor. They would forever be known as the Order of the Cat."

"The Order of the Cat? That doesn't sound too tough," I said.

"You'd be surprised, Marc, at how tough a cat is," replied Millenia. "Cats were sacred animals in ancient Egypt, partly because they could defeat a most fearsome enemy: the snake."

"Wow," I said. "I guess so. But why are you telling me this?"

"Because you, Marc John Jefferies, are a member of that order."

My mouth dropped open. I could not believe my

ears.

"Excuse me," I gasped.

"You are descended from the Order of the Cat," he said. "And your time has come. The world needs you."

"But I'm just a kid," I said. "What can I do?"

"Remember, Marc," he responded. "All of those brilliant students were kids, too. Most were your age. Some were even younger. But that is exactly why we need you."

His voice grew calmer as he spoke.

"Children are brilliant," he continued. "They have marvelous ideas. They learn so many things so quickly."

"You've never seen my report card," I said.

"But we have watched you teach adults how to do things on a computer," said Millenia. "Your grasp of technology is amazing. And we've seen you run faster and climb higher than many adults. You can go places where adults cannot, and sometimes, many times where you are needed, no one is suspicious. And never forget your origins. You come from that brilliant line that first comprised the Order of the Cat. You, Marc John Jefferies, are the perfect secret agent."

I was still in shock.

"But I'm an actor," I said. "I don't have time for this. Glen, tell him"

Glen looked at me and smiled.

"The movies are a cover," Glen said. "We can go on

location wherever there's trouble and no one will know the difference. Don't worry. You'll have time. I'll see to it."

"You mean..."

"That's right," Glen interrupted me. "I'm a member too."

I could not believe it. I was a secret agent. And I was only thirteen!

"This isn't happening," I said. "Glen, is this some kind of joke?"

"Nope," he replied. "It's for real."

"Do my parents know?" I asked.

"Oh no," replied Millenia. "They don't."

"But you said that I was descended from the Order of the Cat. That means that it's in my family, right?" I replied.

"That's right," said Millenia. "But there's more to it."

"Like what?" I asked.

"Everyone needs teachers, Marc John Jefferies," he explained. No, you mustn't tell your parents. They have their own special role. Knowing this is not their path."

"But this is important," I said. "This is big. They've got to know."

"They know enough," said Millenia. "They know that you're not an ordinary kid. They see how smart you are, and they see your talents. And this is precisely why we cannot tell them. They've done their job by bringing you to this point. If we let them know anything else, it could change everything."

"We call them Keepers," said Glen.

"What's a Keeper?" I asked.

Millenia responded immediately.

"So many questions," he marveled. "We skip a generation so that the members of the order do not lose their way. These honored ones, the Keepers, have a great responsibility: it is to raise you and educate you, the chosen few. It brings us great pain that we can not tell or thank them. But it is the only way. Do you understand, Marc?"

It was a lot to take in. My head was spinning, but it all made sense. I nodded yes again.

"I understand," I said. "But I still can't believe it. I still can't believe that I'm a secret agent who's supposed to protect the world!"

Glen looked to the silhouette of Millenia and then back to me again.

"Believe it," said Glen. "Because the world can't wait."

Millenia laughed again. I was getting used to it by now. I shrugged my shoulders.

"So what do I do first?" I asked.

"Why, save the world," replied Millenia. "Nothing more."

And he laughed some more.

Act 4:

SPY GAMES, SPY GEAR

So there I was, seated in Glen's trailer talking to a shadow on the wall about how it was my new job to save the world; about how I, Marc John Jefferies, am descended from a respected and secret crime fighting organization called the Order of the Cat; about how my parents could never know; and finally, about how a thirteen year old kid from the Bronx could change the world. If it happened to you, would you believe it all? I didn't think so.

But still, Glen was a trusted friend. He was a strange friend, but trusted, and I decided that I would listen to what he had to say. And if this was my role, my job in this world, then I needed to accept the responsibility. After all, according to Millenia, the world needed me, and I couldn't take the chance of letting it down.

"Glen," said the silhouette. "Take Marc and have

him outfitted. Then introduce him to his partner."

"Prepschool?" said Glen.

"The one and only," responded Millenia before addressing me. "Marc, you will be going to the small island nation of Cajah Cajah. The princess of the ruling family has gone missing. Her family has kept peace between the neighboring tribes for centuries, and without her, they may soon go to war. Your mission is to find her, and return stability to the lands of the islanders. Good luck, Marc John Jefferies. May victory smile upon you."

And with that, the figure disappeared from the screen, and the POKEY went dark. Glen walked out of the lit area and disappeared into the dark room. A moment later, all of the lights came back on. My eyes had a hard time adjusting, but that did not stop me from asking a few more questions.

"Why do they call him Millenia?"

"No one knows," said Glen. "Some people believe that he is thousands of years old. But that's just a rumor. Be careful of what you hear."

"Are both of my parents Keepers?" I asked.

"Yes, they are," replied Glen. "It's rather extraordinary. In fact, it's never happened before."

"Never?" I asked.

"Never," said Glen. "You're different, Marc. Get used to it. Now, let's get you geared up. Oh, but first, here."

He reached into his pocket and handed me a tiny pin. On it was a claw and a picture of a cattail: the reedy plant that grows along the River Nile.

"That's our symbol," he said. "You can always tell a member of the order by that pin."

We left Glen's trailer, hopped into a Jeep parked outside, and drove across the set. My education was just beginning.

After a couple of twists and turns, we drove up to yet another trailer. From the outside it looked like all the others on the set: metal paneling and a few tiny windows. But it sat slightly away from everything else around it, and although I had never been to this particular trailer before, I had a hunch that I would get to know it well.

We hopped out of the Jeep and bounded up to the entrance. Glen pulled a key from his pocket and unlocked the door. He stepped in ahead of me and I followed.

Clap, clap!

Glen smacked his hands together twice and the lights came on.

"I love that," Glen said. "So, what do we need for this mission?"

"I don't know," I replied shrugging my shoulders. "I've never been a 13 year old secret agent before."

"Good point," said Glen. "Maybe we should start

24

from the ground up. I believe that means shoes."

Glen went to one of the cabinets that hung over the sink at the far end of the room and opened it. The shelves inside were stacked neatly with rows of Spam.

"Flip, flip," said Glen.

The shelves quickly spun around showing a new set of shelves and stacks of boxes of Converse sneakers.

"Whoa," was all I could manage to say.

Glen scanned the boxes moving his index finger over each one.

"Ah hah!" he exclaimed. "These should be your size."

He pulled the box from the stack, set it on the counter, and took the top off.

"Flip, flip," said Glen again, and the shelves spun once more, this time replacing the Cons with the stacks of Spam.

"What is flip, flip?" I asked.

"Oh, yes," Glen said. "I forgot. There are quite a few hiding places for gear on the set, amongst other spots. If you say 'flip,flip,' they should open for you. But make certain that no one is around when you do so. You don't want to give away a secret like that."

Glen turned back to the shoe box, reached inside, pulled out a pair of new Converse sneakers, and held them out to me.

"Here," Glen said. "Put these on."

"But I have a pair of Converse already," I protested. "Everybody's got a pair."

"Not like these," Glen responded smiling. "Trust me. Put them on."

There was a chair by the door, and unlike my trailer or Glen's trailer, it wasn't covered with stuff. I went to it, sat down, took off my shoes, and put on the new sneakers. They fit perfectly.

"Now," said Glen. "Step over here."

He pointed to a place on the floor. A red bull's eye target was painted there and directly above it, on the ceiling, was painted another. I walked over to the target on the floor and stood on it. Glen stood next to me.

"Flip, flip," he said.

The bull's eye overhead slid aside opening a hole in the ceiling and revealing the clear, blue sky above.

"Now," said Glen. "Step up on your tippy toes."

I tiptoed, balancing in place.

"And then jump straight up," he continued.

"Why?" I asked.

"Just try," Glen urged.

"Okay," was all that I could say. This was not a very comfortable jumping position, but I put my arms down at my sides and jumped.

I took off like a rocket!

I went straight up, through the roof, twenty feet

into the air. I caught a quick glimpse of the set. Everyone was still eating lunch, and no one even noticed me!

I fell back into the trailer and landed softly on my feet without a scratch. The cushion in the shoes that bounced me into the sky was now like a featherbed under my feet.

"Wow!" I exclaimed. "These shoes are awesome."

"Flip, flip," said Glen, and the hole closed.

"What are these?" I asked.

"A new Converse with ultra jump technology: a bouncy substance that gives you another twenty feet on your leaping distance," explained Glen.

"I can dunk now," I said happily.

"Yes, Marc John Jefferies, you can," said Glen. "But you mustn't. People will get suspicious."

I looked down at the new shoes.

'We'd see about that,' I thought. As soon as Glen was gone, I was going to hit the court.

"Remember," said Glen. "Tiptoes are the key."

He went to another cabinet on the other side of the room and opened it. This one was empty.

"Flip, flip," Glen said.

The shelves spun like the others and boxes of cell phones appeared. Glen pulled one from the stack.

"Flip, flip," I called from across the room, and the shelves spun back. Glen smiled.

"Please, Marc," he said. "Not until I'm ready."

"Were you ready?" I replied.

"Well, yes," Glen said. "Anyway, here."

He handed me a tiny cell phone just like the one that he had given me earlier.

"My parent's got me a cell phone for emergencies only," I told him. "I don't need another one."

"Oh, this one is for emergencies all right," replied Glen. "And you will need it. It has a built in GPS tracking system that is connected to a panic button. Press that button and someone will be around with a helicopter within five minutes to pick you up and take you to safety or wherever it is that you need to go. We call it the Loop."

Glen then walked over to an overstuffed chair that sat near a window. He pulled off the cushion, and then issued his command.

"Flip, flip," he said.

The pad underneath rolled over revealing what appeared to be a drinking straw.

"You'll definitely need this Bubble Stick," Glen said.

"Why, so I can drink a Coke?" I laughed. "Besides, I'm not using some straw that you found under a cushion."

"Very funny," said Glen with a serious look. "The Bubble Stick only looks like a straw, but it has a miniature filtration device installed within it so that you can breathe underwater. But don't try to breathe underwater with a regular straw or you'll soon find yourself in trouble. And don't lose that one. Now, where is that last device?"

Glen again appeared to be lost. He walked around the room twice, and eventually stopped in front of a small refrigerator. He opened the door, reached inside, and pulled a watch from the top shelf.

"Here you go, Marc," said Glen handing me the funky looking timepiece. "This should do it."

I took the watch from him and put it on my wrist. It had a swirled blue pattern on the face and a clear band.

"What does this do?" I asked. "Wait a minute, I know. It makes me invisible, right. If I press the button on the side, you won't be able to see me."

I pressed the button.

"You can't see me, can you Glen," I said, impressed with my own cleverness. "What do you call this, Glen? Is it called the I'm Invisible Thing? Maybe it's called the Here Today Gone Today Device."

"Actually Marc, it's called a watch," countered Glen.

"That's a boring name," I replied looking down at it. "What does it do?"

"It tells time, Marc John Jefferies," said Glen. "Being on time is important. Your mother gave it to me a week ago. I just forgot to pass it on to you. She said that you were late twice last week."

"Oh," I mumbled. "You mean I'm not invisible."

"No," responded Glen. "But you might be late again if we don't hurry. What time is it?"

I looked at my watch. Even though it didn't make me invisible, it was still cool looking.

"Eleven fifteen," I said.

"We've got to go," said Glen. "We may still be able to catch your new tutor."

"My new tutor," I exclaimed. "Aw, man. I'm not supposed to go to my tutor until 2 o'clock."

"Plans have changed, Marc," said Glen. "Besides, this is one tutor I think that you'll want to meet."

"What are my parents going to say?" I asked.

"Don't worry about them," said Glen. "I'll take care of everything."

Glen smiled.

"Come on," he said. "It's time to meet Scooter Brosnan. Codename: Prepschool."

Act 5:
A NEW FRIEND

Glen and I climbed into his Jeep and drove away from the set to find some kid named Scooter Brosnan. We were soon on a dirt road heading away from the ocean, the movies, and toward a thick jungle. Palm trees hung over the path and every so often a strange noise from an animal could be heard in the distance.

Suddenly, the brush was gone and as we drove out of the thick of the jungle, I could see the ocean again. The beach looked smooth, but the Jeep bumped along as Glen drove furiously across it. I clutched my cargo pocket to keep the Loop and the Bubble Stick from falling out.

Glen skidded to a stop at the waters edge and it took me a second to recover from the crazy ride. He jumped out of the Jeep and I followed. We walked down to the surf where a tiny rowboat sat waiting.

"Get in," said Glen.

I did as I was told, and Glen shoved the boat into the water, jumping in after I was afloat. He sat on the center bench, grabbed the oars and began to row towards a yacht that was anchored about one hundred feet offshore.

Just as we came up alongside of the ship, a boy of about sixteen appeared from a cabin on board.

"Ahoy, chaps," said the boy.

He was an average sized kid. He wore a blue sport coat and khaki pants with a red and blue striped tie. The boy threw a rope down to us which Glen tied to our rowboat. Then the boy dropped us a rope ladder. Glen held it for me while I climbed up.

I reached the deck of the boat and the boy reached out his hand to help me up.

"Easy. Up and over," said the kid. "There you go, chap."

I could now see him fully. Along with his other clothes, he wore a captain's hat and brown penny loafers with a shiny new penny stuck in the tongue of each one. Glen climbed up behind me.

"Marc John Jefferies," said Glen still huffing and puffing from the rowing and the climb up the ladder. "Meet Scooter Brosnan. Codename: Prepschool."

"Charmed," said Scooter.

He removed his hat revealing strawberry blond hair neatly parted on one side. He reached out his hand for a shake.

"Scooter Brosnan of the Westport, Connecticut Brosnans," he said as I grasped his hand. "Pleased to meet you. Delighted even."

He had a strange snobbishness about him and he spoke as if he ruled the world. Standing side by side, we looked as different from one another as any two people could. I liked him immediately.

"A real New Yorker, are you," said Scooter shaking his head. "An honest to goodness city dweller. Fascinating. Glorious even."

He shook his head some more. He was much shorter than he looked from the rowboat, and I could see that sewn onto his coat was a crest from his school. His shirt was pressed to perfection.

"So, chum," said Scooter as he released my hand. "What's your codename?"

"I don't know," I admitted as I turned to Glen. "What's my codename?"

Glen scratched his head.

"We didn't get that far yet," he said. "We were in such a hurry to catch you Scooter that we never thought of one."

"No need to hurry, sport," said Scooter. "Millenia called ahead and told me that you were coming. Now, Marc, you need a codename. Do you have a nickname by chance?"

Glen smiled.

"Yes he does," said Glen.

"My friends and family call me Boogie," I said.

"What's so funny about that?" asked Scooter.

"I can't dance," I replied. "I mean, I'm really bad at it."

"Then that's perfect, old bean," exclaimed Scooter. "But might I suggest a spin, to make it more fearsome."

"Go for it," I told him.

"How about Boogieman," he said. "Sounds more frightening, doesn't it. That ought to give the Order of the Snake something to think about."

Boogieman. I liked the sound of that.

"The Order of the Snake?" I said. "Scooter, do you think that they had anything to do with the disappearance of Princess...what's her name?"

"Princess Telia," said Scooter. "I don't know. But Millenia told me to clear my schedule so that I could work with you. I guess the SAT test will have to wait."

"Isn't that a test to get into college?" I asked.

"Yes," said Scooter. "But don't worry about me missing it. I've taken it twice already and gotten a perfect score both times. This time was just for fun."

Yes, Scooter was just as strange as Glen, but he was also a genius.

"Marc," said Glen. "Now would be a good time to hit the panic button on the Loop."

I pulled the Loop from my cargo pocket and hit the button.

"You two will be off to the island of Cajah Cajah to meet with the Princess' father, King Letalia," said Glen.

"Excellent play, Glen," said Scooter. "I've been meaning to look the king up. It's been ages since we last had tea."

"Is he a friend of yours?" I asked. "I've never met a king before."

"Squarely so," said Scooter. "Don't worry. He's just a regular sort of fellow. No need to do anything special. Just be yourself, Marc."

A helicopter appeared on the horizon and made its way toward the yacht. The roar of the chopper became louder and louder as it flew closer and closer. Soon it was over head, and Scooter and Glen clutched their caps to keep them from blowing off. Both had to shout to be heard.

"GOOD LUCK!" shouted Glen. "MAY VICTORY SMILE UPON YOU!"

"ARE YOU READY, BOOGIEMAN!" shouted Scooter.

A cable with a hook on the end lowered down to us.

"GRAB ON!" Scooter said.

I took the cable in my hand and held on tightly, and Scooter did the same as he looked at me and shouted:

"LET THE GAME BEGIN!"

The cable pulled us upward toward the waiting helicopter. Glen and the yacht got smaller and smaller as Scooter and I rose higher and higher into the air. This was my first mission as Boogieman: secret agent for the Order of the Cat.

What would come next made life as a movie star seem easy and boring. After all, we were off to meet a king, find a princess, and stop a war. All before lunchtime. Who knew being thirteen would be this interesting.

Act 6:
THE PALACE

The helicopter flew low and fast out across the ocean toward our destination.

"I better phone ahead," said Scooter as he took his Loop from his jacket pocket. "The palace is heavily guarded and the last thing that we need is to be torn apart by the king's men."

Within an hour we had reached Cajah Cajah. There we landed on the front lawn of a massive palace surrounded by lavish gardens and enclosed within a twelve foot high stone wall. Just as Scooter had said, the place was heavily guarded but not in a way you could possibly imagine. Everywhere I looked was a wondrous sight. Men rode near the perimeter fence atop elephants while others lead tigers near the front gate.

"Got it," said Scooter into the Loop before putting it back in his pocket. "That was Johnny in Tower B. He said that we were clear to land."

The helicopter set down, and no sooner had we leapt from it than it took flight, once more disappearing beyond the horizon.

None of the guards paid any attention to us as we walked right up to the front door, opened it, and walked inside.

"Scooter," I said. "How did you know who to call?"

"See, Marcus, my dear friend," he said. "King Letalia and my family go way back. This is not the first time that I've been to this palace. You'll see. But don't forget though, not a word about our mission. Like everyone else, his Highness has no idea about our belonging to the Order of the Cat. It's rather interesting."

"Why is that interesting?" I asked.

"Well," began Scooter. "If my Order of the Cat history is correct, and indeed it is, this palace was built by the Order a couple of hundred years ago as a gift to the royal family."

"What was the gift for?" I asked.

"You are full of questions, aren't you," said Scooter shaking his head. "I like that. It was a gift for a favor that the royal family had done for the Order. But to be honest, I can't remember the favor. It's not important."

I nodded my head to show that I understood, and I continued to follow Scooter through the halls of this wondrous place.

The walls were trimmed with gold, and paintings hung everywhere. Sculptures lined the walkways alongside of varieties of exotic plants. Although it was full of art and treasure, the palace was oddly devoid of people.

We soon entered a great ballroom with fifty foot ceilings. The roof was held up by enormous marble columns while great crystal chandeliers hung down from the center.

"Scooter, my boy!" came a voice from the far end of the room. "Over here."

"Your Highness," answered Scooter as he began to trek across the massive room.

Scooter reached the king and they shook hands.

He was a little man, shorter than my thirteen year old self, and he couldn't have been a day over thirty-five; a young age for a king. But he looked the part wearing royal purple robes and a crown speckled with jewels.

"What brings you to Cajah Cajah?" asked the king.

"I'm helping a new friend with his studies while he shoots a movie on a nearby island," replied Scooter being careful not to give away our mission. "My father said that while I was here I should stop by and say hello. King Letalia, let me introduce to you Marc John Jefferies."

"Marc John Jefferies," said the king. His eyes lit up

with excitement. "My daughter has seen all of your movies."

He reached out and grabbed my hand shaking it excitedly. He suddenly stopped, pulled a handkerchief from his robe and held it up to his eyes, slowly wiping away newly formed tears.

"I'm sorry, Marc. I don't mean to cry. In fact, I wish Princess Telia could be here to meet you herself, but alas," said the king, "she's gone missing."

"What happened sir?" asked Scooter.

"I do not know," said the king. "Three days ago we went to a peace council with the two neighboring tribes of Dontala and Rontala. As you know, our family has kept peace between the tribes for centuries. When we heard that they were about to go to war again, we went to them immediately to stop it. They took a special liking to Telia and peace was made, again. We returned home, and Telia went to her room for a nap. A moment later, I heard a scream, and when I went to her chamber, she was gone."

"And no one has seen her since?" I asked.

"No one," said the king.

"What were the two tribes fighting about?" asked Scooter.

"It seems that a scientist by the name of Dr. Foulton had discovered two special plants: one of them grows on Dontala and the other on Rontala," recounted the king. "When combined, these two plants can take the salt out of sea water and make it fresh. And as you know, finding fresh water here is difficult. Both kingdoms, untrusting, accused each other of stealing one another's plants and plotting to sell them without sharing the profit with the other. They could both benefit if they worked together. Telia had come close to convincing them of this right before she disappeared. With her gone, I fear that the peace is only temporary."

"Do you think that one of the tribes kidnapped her?" I asked.

"Oh, no," replied the king. "They loved my daughter. But surely, if they find out that she is missing, they will accuse each other of her disappearance. I fear that without her, war will surely come to the region."

"Dear King," said Scooter, "Have you yet told anyone of her disappearance?"

"Just the palace police, but no one else," said the King. "And they've found nothing. But the secret will not keep long. Now, if you'll forgive me boys, I'm very distraught and tired, and I need to lie down. Please excuse me. But do make yourselves comfortable in the palace. A friend of yours, Scooter, is a friend of mine. Nice meeting you, Marc."

"You too," I said and waved to the King as he left the room.

"We must find the princess before it is too late,"

said Scooter.

"Where do we begin?" I asked.

"Let's check her room," said Scooter. "That's the last place that she was heard from. Maybe it holds a clue."

"Lead the way," I said. "You're the one who's been here before."

Scooter ran back to the entrance of the palace and up the grand marble staircase that was there. I followed close behind.

We reached the top and we looked down what appeared to be an endless hallway. I could see hundreds of doors.

"Goodness me," said Scooter. "Marc, my friend, I've forgotten which room is hers. Now what?"

I slowly walked down the hall, looking at each of the identical entrances. About twenty feet down, I stopped.

"How about this one," I said.

Scooter approached, took one look and laughed.

"Jolly good show, Marc," he exclaimed. "And all it took was a little common sense."

On the door in front of us in swirled letters was a sign. It read:

Princess Telia.

"My turn to lead," I said.

And we went inside to check for clues.

Act 7:
THE PASSAGE

Princess Telia's room was massive. A giant canopy bed sat in the middle of the cavernous pink abode, dolls and stuffed toys were everywhere. A picture of she and her father, King Letalia, sat neatly on top of her desk. Scooter went over to it.

"Where shall we start, my friend?" asked Scooter as he picked-up the photo and examined it.

"You know better than I," I reminded him. "This is, after all, my first mission."

"Steady observation, Boogieman," replied Scooter. "I say that we search the place from top to bottom: in the drawers, the closet, under the bed, in her shoes..."

Scooter went on to list every possible place that could hold anything including the cracks in the floor, and while he rambled on, I took a quick look around the place. The window was open. I went to it and looked out over the kingdom.

Land stretched out before me to the sea. In the distance I could see two identical little islands that must have been Dontala and Rontala. I turned back to the room to help with the search.

"So," began Scooter. "What do you think so far?"

"Of what?" I asked.

"The Order of the Cat," he responded. "Being an agent. What do you think?"

"It's a lot to take in," I responded.

"It is," he said. "But you're doing something very important. And it can be fun."

"That 'flip, flip' thing is pretty cool," I said with a smile.

"That it is..."

Scooter's voice trailed off when a scraping sound was heard. I looked toward its source. It was coming from the closet. I ran over, opened the door, and looked inside.

"Check this out," I said to Scooter.

His eyes widened as he crossed towards me and peered over my shoulder.

"Gracious," he said. "How can that be?"

In front of us was a passageway. Steps led down into a lit corridor and disappeared around a corner.

"Where did that come from?" Scooter asked.

"Flip, flip," I said again.

The passage way began to close as a closet lowered back down into its place.

"Flip, flip," I said once more.

The clothes disappeared, and the passageway reopened.

"Well," I said. "You did say that this place was built by the Order of the Cat."

"But who would have known this was here?" asked Scooter.

"A member of the Order," I said.

"Not possible," said Scooter. "No one in the Order of the Cat would have taken the princess. Besides, we don't even know if this passage has anything to do with her disappearance."

"There's only one way to find out," I said. "Follow me."

And I walked down into the passage. When Scooter was inside, I said the words again.

"Flip, flip."

The passage way closed, and we continued on. After we turned the corner at the bottom of the steps, the passage straightened out. We followed it for several hundred yards, when suddenly, I spotted something shiny lying on the floor. I bent down and picked-up a tiny ruby ring. The stone was huge!

"That belonged to the princess," said Scooter.

"How do you know?" I asked.

"I was at her last birthday party when her father gave it to her," he said. "She always wore it. I am now certain that she has been kidnapped. She would not have let that out of her sight."

"Then she definitely came this way," I said. "Which leaves more questions than answers."

We continued to walk until the tunnel came to a dead end.

"Flip, flip," I said.

The wall spun around, and bright sunlight poured in. I had to cover my eyes for a moment before walking out of the passage. The ocean lapped before us, and when I turned around I could see that we were standing at the base of a rock cliff. High above us was the castle wall.

"We're on the other side of the island," said Scooter.

"Now what?" I asked.

"We need to report back to Millenia," said Scooter. "And figure out who did this."

I pulled the Loop from my pocket and hit the panic button. A moment later, a helicopter appeared and set down gently on the beach.

"Flip, flip," I said, and the secret passageway closed once more leaving what appeared to be nothing more than stone in its place.

Our mission, it seemed, just got harder.

Act 8:
CHECKING IN

Scooter and I returned to the movie set and met with Glen. We quickly explained how we had found the passageway and the ring. Glen seemed puzzled.

"That does sound odd," said Glen. "Who outside of the Order of the Cat would know that the passage was there?"

"We asked the same question," I said. "What does Millenia have to say about it?"

"I don't know," said Glen. "Let's ask."

He produced the POKEY, lowered the shades, and...

Clap! Clap!

The room went dark, a light shot out from the POKEY and Millenia's figure appeared on the wall.

"Greetings, all," said the shadow. "What news

do you bring?"

Glen shared our discovery with the mysterious figure. Millenia said nothing.

"Well," said Glen. "Any ideas?"

There was silence and then Millenia spoke.

"No," he said.

We all looked at one another. That was a rather short answer to such a complex question. We shook it off and continued.

"What next, sir?" asked Scooter.

"Marc, you and Scooter need to visit the islands of Rontala and Dontala. Go see what you can find," said Millenia. "But be cautious. The islanders of both tribes are very welcoming, but suspicious."

"Don't worry, sir," said Scooter. "My island history is top notch."

"Good," said Millenia. "Good luck, and may victory smile upon you."

And Millenia's shadow disappeared.

"You heard the man," said Glen. "My Jeep is outside. I'll take you to the boat."

"Can I drive, chap?" asked Scooter with hesitancy.

"No," said Glen. "I've got it."

"I insist," said Scooter.

"Please," I begged Glen. "Let him drive."

"Why?" asked Glen perplexed. "What's wrong

with my driving?"

"It's a little bumpy," I said. "You drive well, but you're just a little..."

"Oh, say it," said Scooter. "His driving's awful."

Glen was silent for a moment.

"No offense," said Scooter.

"None taken," said Glen. "You're right. My driving is awful."

Glen smiled and then tossed the keys to Scooter.

"Front seat!" I exclaimed.

"Darn," said Glen snapping his fingers.

"Sorry, chum," said Scooter. "Better luck next time.

And we ran outside to our ride.

Act 9:
ENGLISH PRINCESSES

We drove out to the oceanfront where Glen left us on the sandy beach.

"Remember," Glen warned us. "The islanders are very friendly, but also very complex."

"Don't worry, chief," said Scooter. "I'll take care of it."

Glen drove away as Scooter and I climbed into a small boat with a motor.

"What does Glen mean by complex?" I asked.

"Many people have been coming to Rontala for a long time," said Scooter. "They come for all sorts of reasons: backpackers, adventurers, scientists. And the Rontalians are very kind, but they are also very complex. Take their language for example. No one, not even a Rontalian, can speak fluent Rontalish."

"They can't even speak their own language?" I said in disbelief. "How odd."

"And it's not because they're stupid, Marc," continued Scooter. "In fact, they're all quite brilliant. But the language has so many words and rules...it just goes on and on. It's simply too complex, for anyone."

Scooter started the motor and we sped out across the water toward Rontala. Within a matter of minutes we pulled up onto the beach.

We dragged the boat onto the shore and began the walk to the village. All along our path windmills could be seen towering above the trees.

"Power sources," said Scooter with a smile. "Completely clean, chap. No pollution from the windmills. Absolutely brilliant."

"That doesn't seem so complex," I said.

"Well, if you were to look inside, Marcus, you'd find a giant mess of gears," he finished. "We might only use two or three gears in a contraption like that, but a Rontalian would use ten or twelve. Everything is complex here."

We entered a particularly thick part of the jungle on the island, and after walking for another ten minutes, we came upon a clearing. There stood a village.

Grass huts were everywhere. People ran about doing work, and children played. We walked further in, and as we did so, a crowd began to form around us. Each person stared at us as we walked, but said nothing.

"Hello," I said, but no one responded.

"No use," said Scooter. "Chances are none of them speak English. If there is one thing harder than speaking Rontalian, it is translating Rontalian to another language. We'll need to find the village elder if we want to talk with someone. Just smile and wave."

I did so and in return, everyone in the crowd responded with a smile and a wave of his or her own. Friendly people.

We came to a well and on its edge sat a fragile old man. He had white hair and wore loose clothes. A group sat on the ground before him.

"That's our man," said Scooter. "Greetings," Scooter called out to him.

The elder looked up at us and smiled.

"Do you speak English?" asked Scooter.

"You are English?" asked the elder.

"Close enough," said Scooter.

"No, we speak English," I said.

The man smiled.

"Ah, good," said the elder. "You are English."

"No," I protested. "We speak English."

"Forget it, chum," said Scooter to me. "Our language is too simple. Remember, complex. Just run with it."

I smiled.

"Have you seen the princess lately?" asked Scooter.

The man smiled and then addressed the crowd in Rontalish. Everyone around us began to bow and smile.

"Have you?" asked Scooter.

"The people of Rontala are very pleased to have two English princesses on the island," said the man. "Thank you for coming."

"But we're not English princesses," I protested. "We're looking for Princess Telia. Have you seen her?"

"You are not Princess Telia," said the elder. "I have seen Princess Telia and you are not her."

"No, that is right," I said. "We are looking for the princess. She is missing."

The man quickly addressed the crowd. They responded with excited murmurs and then applause. The elder addressed us.

"The people of Rontala are fascinated that you two English princesses can be missing and here at the same time," said the elder. "They feel that you must be very special people."

Scooter turned to me.

"Do you see why it takes so long to negotiate with the islands," said Scooter to me.

"This is silly," I said.

"No, pal of mine, not silly," responded Scooter. "Just complex. Trust me."

"No," I responded. "This is silly." I said it louder.

"This is silly!"

"No," said the elder. "Silly is being able to fly without wings."

The elder then addressed his people in Rontalish. They all laughed.

"Hey," I said. "You understand silly."

"Yes I understand silly," said the elder. "The thought of silly is a very complex thing."

I turned to Scooter.

"No it isn't," I said. "Silly is very simple. Scooter, they understand silly. Watch."

I stepped up on my tip-toes.

"Marc," said Scooter. "What are you doing?"

"They think flying is silly," I said. "So, I'm going to do something silly. They'll like it."

"Marc," said Scooter. "I don't think that..."

But before he could finish, I jumped into the air, sailing twenty feet overhead with the help of my Cons with ultrajump technology. I then came down, landing easily on the sand. I looked at the faces of the islanders. Every mouth was agape. Every eye was wide open. No one said a word. Suddenly, without warning, they all ran.

People dove for nearby houses. Doors slammed shut. Window shutters were closed, and as quickly as I had jumped, the entire village had disappeared. Everyone that is, except for one. The village elder stood shaking in front of the well.

"What happened?" I asked. "I thought that flying without wings was silly."

"Flying without wings is silly," said the elder. "Flying without wings is also unnatural and very scary."

He stood for a moment and then suddenly ran, escaping into a nearby home.

"I don't understand," I said. "What did I do?"

"You got me, buddy," said Scooter. "Like I said, these are very complex people. Come on, let's go to Dontala. Maybe our luck will be better there."

"But..." I said.

"Maybe you better leave all of the talking to me, chap," said Scooter. "Just until you get the hang of the secret agent business."

Maybe Scooter had a good point.

"Good idea," I said slowly. I hung my head low. "I was just being silly."

"Actors," said Scooter with a smile. I looked up and when I saw him, we both began to laugh.

"On to Dontala!"

We ran back to the boat and climbed aboard. It was getting late and the sun was rapidly setting. While Scooter started the motor getting ready to drive us back toward the movie set, I called Glen on the Loop to give him an update. He laughed when I told him about the flying episode.

"That is pretty funny," said Glen.

"Maybe," I told him. "But it doesn't help us to find the princess."

"I guess not," said Glen. "How did the people seem? Were they happy?"

"Oh, yes," I said. "They were very happy."

"Good," he replied. "They probably don't even know that she's missing yet. Better luck at Dontala."

"Thanks," I said. "But it's late. I think that we'll wait until tomorrow to go."

"Good idea," said Glen.

"What about the movie?" I asked. "Can I miss tomorrow?"

"Not a problem," said Glen. "We'll just shoot some of the scenes that you're not in. Oh, and Marc."

"Yes," I replied.

"Better let Scooter do all of the talking this time," said Glen.

I sighed.

"Agent Boogieman out," I said and hung up. I turned to Scooter. "A guy makes one mistake..."

Scooter looked at me with a confused face.

"Nevermind," I said with a smile.

Scooter chuckled, revved the motor and carried us off toward home.

Act 10:
CAPTURED

We left early the next morning at sunrise. My dad and mom were having coffee when I was trying to leave the hotel room.

"Where are you off to so early?" asked my Dad.

"Sightseeing," I said.

"Well, have fun," said my mother. "And be careful."

If she only knew.

I ran out of the room and down to the shoreline where Scooter sat waiting in our boat.

"Another day, my friend," said Scooter. "Are you ready for some more adventure?"

"Why not," I said as we sped away out over the water.

When we reached the island of Dontala, a group of islanders had already gathered on the shore. Several ran into the water and helped to pull our boat onto the beach.

"Friendly welcome, eh Marcus," said Scooter grinning. "Almost as if they were expecting us."

I looked around. No one was smiling. Instead, everyone stared at us with an angry expression.

"Scooter, I don't know if we should get out of the boat," I said nervously. "This doesn't seem right."

"Nonsense," said Scooter jumping from the vessel and running onto shore. "Come on."

I slowly climbed out of the boat and walked toward Scooter.

"Greetings," said Scooter with a smile.

Suddenly, the crowd rushed towards us and jumped on us.

"See, Marc," said Scooter. "They're hugging us."

"What are you doing?" I demanded.

The men said nothing. Instead, one of the islanders produced some rope. A giant of a man held me while another tied my hands and legs. I struggled, but it was no use. These guys were just too big. One of the men suddenly threw me over his shoulder.

"Where are you taking us?" I demanded, but the man said nothing. "Scooter," I called out. "What's this all about?"

"Maybe it's a new custom," said Scooter.

"A new custom!" I exclaimed.

"Possibly," he said.

"A moment ago you couldn't tell the difference between a hug and a tackle!" I said.

"Marc, I am a genius, but I have been known to be wrong from time to time," said Scooter. Then he paused. "Well, actually, I've only been wrong once and that was not my fault."

I turned my head and saw that Scooter was also tied up and strung over someone's shoulder. The men began to carry us away from the shore and toward the center of the island. They walked onto a jungle trail that was very much like the one we had traveled on Rontala. The brush was just as thick and my head bounced off of one or two tree branches along the way.

"Excuse me," I said to my captors. "Could you please be more careful?"

"Marc," Scooter responded. "I thought that I was going to do all of the talking this time."

"Well then, talk," I urged.

"Excuse me," said Scooter. "Could you please be more careful?"

"Thanks," I said. I addressed the silent men. "Where are you taking us?" I demanded once more.

Still they said nothing.

"Scooter," I said. "Why won't they answer me? Don't they understand?"

"Maybe they don't," said Scooter.

"Quiet," said one of the men. "No talking."

"You do understand!" I exclaimed.

"Of course we understand," said the man. "What do you think this is, Rontala?"

"Where are you taking us?" I demanded again.

The man stopped and everyone else did the same thing. He turned toward me.

"Silence," he said.

"But I want to know..."

"Too many questions!" said the man.

He took a short piece of rope and gagged my mouth. He then looked me in the eye.

"You are going to see the chief," said the man. "He will tell you all that you need to know."

We bumped along, Scooter staying hushed and me with a piece of foul tasting rope in my mouth.

The men paraded us through town. As we passed, people pointed and talked to one another with astonishment. The village looked exactly the same as the one on Rontala. The people dressed the same. A village elder was even perched on a well in the center of town with a small crowd surrounding him. Everything was exactly the same. Well, almost everything. No one had bound and gagged me on Rontala.

We approached a small hut. Everyone stopped except for the two men who carried Scooter and me. They took us inside and dropped us on the ground. Another man approached, bent down to me and untied my mouth.

"Finally," I said.

"Silence!" commanded a voice. "Invaders will not speak!"

I looked up. There sat a woman wearing a crown. She was plain looking but stern. Her hair was pinned straight and black. She held a staff in one hand.

"We're not invaders," I said.

"Lies!" she said. "Our spies saw the people of Rontala bowing down to you, and I, the Queen of Dontala know that you must be their new leader."

"You're mistaken, Madam," said Scooter. "You see..."

"Silence!" she commanded. "We know what we saw."

"But it was a mistake," I pleaded. "You see..."

"We know what we saw!" she said again, this time more forcefully.

"If you just talk to the people of Rontala, they'll straighten the whole thing out," I said.

Everyone in the room, including the Queen, began to laugh.

"Talk to the people of Rontala," she said with a giggle. "Who can understand them? They are too complex, too confusing. And so are you. You are trying to confuse me with your lies."

"No," I said. "We are trying to tell you the truth. We're here looking for Princess Telia."

"More lies!" said the Queen. "You have come to invade us. You have come to take our plants."

"No!" I responded.

"There is only one way to deal with invaders," she said.

The people in the room began to chant.

"Jot-cha. Jot-cha. Jot-cha."

"Jotcha!" exclaimed the Queen and everyone cheered.

"Hooray!" exclaimed the people.

Two men ran over to us, scooped us up, took us out of the room and into the street. They held us over their heads. The Queen came out as well and stepped in front of us to address the village.

"People of Dontala!" she called. A crowd assembled. "Today, we have captured two invaders from Rontala."

"Hooray!" exclaimed the crowd.

"And we all know how to handle invaders!"

The crowd chanted.

"Jot-cha! Jot-cha! Jot-cha!"

"Jotcha!" cried the Queen.

"Hooray!" exclaimed the people.

"Scooter," I said. "What is Jotcha?"

"Jotcha," said Scooter. "They wouldn't."

"Scooter," I said. "What is it?"

"Jotcha is an ancient ritual that hasn't been performed for hundreds of years," he said.

"What is it?!" I demanded.

Scooter turned his head toward me. His face was serious.

"I believe, Marc, my friend," he said with a gulp. "That we're going to be fed to a sea monster."

"A sea monster," I said with a chuckle. "You must be wrong again."

"Jot-cha! Jot-cha! Jot-cha!" chanted the people.

"Jotcha!" cried the Queen.

"Unfortunately, Marc," said Scooter. "I am one hundred percent correct.

The Queen turned toward us. Her eyes gleamed with anticipation.

"Dinnertime!" she said to us.

And the crowd ran down toward the beach with us still held high in the air.

"Jotcha!"

Act 11:
DINNER HOUR ESCAPE

Being a secret agent wasn't turning out the way that I had expected it to. So far, I had scared an innocent island full of people and been mistaken as an invader. Now, I was about to be fed to a sea monster.

"What does this sea monster look like?" I asked Scooter.

"I don't know," he responded. "I've never read a description of it. I just know that it's ferocious and feared by the people of the island of Dontala."

"Well, what's going to happen next?" I asked.

"Silence!" called the Queen. She smiled. "You will see soon enough."

The villagers carried us down to the shore. Two people were already standing there pounding large posts into the sand. The men carrying us flopped us onto the sand and began to tie another rope to the posts. Then they tied that rope to our feet and walked back over to stand next to the queen.

"Who will be brave enough to watch over the prisoners and call out the sighting of Jotcha?" she asked.

A small child stepped forward. She was tiny. I suspect that she was about five years old.

"I'll do it," she said. "I'll call Jotcha."

"Is no one else as brave as this child?" asked the Queen.

No one answered.

"Very well," she said. She bent down to address the girl. "Do you know what to do?"

The little girl nodded yes.

"Very good," said the queen.

"Jot-cha. Jot-cha. Jot-cha." chanted the crowd.

"Jotcha!" exclaimed the queen as she stood.

"Hooray!" exclaimed the crowd as they all left. All except for the little girl.

She stood over us, waiting to call 'Jotcha.'

"Now what?" I asked Scooter.

"Now we wait," he replied.

"Wait for what?" I asked.

"To be eaten," he said calmly.

"Ah," I responded.

I struggled to free my hands, but I could not. Then, I rolled over to look at the little girl.

"Excuse me," I said.

She stared at me but said nothing.

"Would you please untie us so that we can go home?" I asked her in my sweetest, kindest voice.

"I can't," she said. "You have to stay here and wait for Jotcha."

"Well," I said. "If you untie me, I promise that I'll stay here and wait for Jotcha."

"Okay," she said.

Scooter rolled over and looked at me. His eyes were open wide in disbelief as the little girl came over and began to untie my hands.

"That's it," he said with a shocked voice. "You make a promise to stay here and she just does what you ask?"

"Of course," I said as the little girl finished loosening my hands. I looked at her. "We always have to keep our promises."

The little girl nodded in agreement. I turned to Scooter.

"I have a little sister," I said. "Works everytime."

"Jotcha!" screamed the little girl suddenly pointing to the water's edge. "Jotcha!"

"Where?" I asked frantically.

She pointed to the water.

"A bump in the water!" she exclaimed. "Jotcha!"

She ran away, back toward the village, as fast as she could. I started to untie my feet as quickly as I could, all of the while looking over my shoulder. A small bump appeared at the edge of the shore.

"Better make it quick, chap," said Scooter. "I think that I see a head."

"I'm trying," I said.

I finished untying my hands and went to work on Scooter's bonds.

"Hurry!" he urged.

I freed his hands and then tried to untie his feet but the knots were too tight.

"They're not coming undone!" I said.

"It's coming out of the water, old bean!" exclaimed Scooter.

I turned toward the water and stared. There it was, moving slowly out of the water, but the bump never got any bigger. Instead, it just got closer. It seemed to be an awfully tiny sea monster. I stopped what I was doing. The thing looked oddly familiar. I stood and left Scooter.

"Where are you going?" he asked nervously going back to work on his bonds.

I began to walk toward the water's edge. The sea monster had stopped moving as the waves washed over it. Suddenly, a swell larger than the others came crashing into the shore. I jumped back to keep from getting wet. The water rushed nearly up to my feet pushing the sea monster up on shore. When the water receded, the mystery was solved. I laughed out loud.

"What's so funny," said Scooter who had finally

untied himself and run down to join me.

I pointed down at the sand. Scooter smiled and slowly broke into a fit of laughter.

"Jotcha," he said.

"Jotcha," I said back to him.

There in front of us lay an old sea turtle. I bent down for a closer look and its head disappeared into its shell.

"Now I remember," said Scooter. "Turtle wor-shippers."

I turned to look at Scooter.

"Now you remember," I said sarcastically.

"The people of the island are afraid of turtles," said Scooter.

"Why?" I asked.

"Why is Rontalish such a complex language?" he replied. "No one knows."

I looked back to the turtle before pulling the Loop from my pocket and hitting the panic button. I then put the Loop away and waited for our ride.

"Jotcha," I said again, slowly shaking my head.

The turtle poked its head back out, turned around in the sand and made the slow trek back toward the water.

Act 12:
NEW DIRECTIONS

Scooter and I flew back to the set with no new evidence that would help us find the princess. The islands had been of no help, and it would only be a matter of time before they went to war with one another.

The next day, we met Glen in his trailer for a briefing. When we arrived, Millenia was already projected onto the screen.

"Greetings, crime fighters," said Millenia. "What news do you bring?"

"Nothing new, sir," said Scooter. "But we were almost eaten by a turtle."

"I see," said Millenia. "Jotcha."

"What is Jotcha?" asked Glen.

Scooter quickly explained the ritual and what happened to us on Dontala. He also recounted the story of how I helped us to escape.

"Good work, Agent Boogieman," said Millenia. "Quick thinking."

"Right. Quick thinking," I said. "But we still haven't found the princess. Time is running out."

"Patience, Marc," said Millenia. "You must keep trying."

"I don't know, Millenia," I replied. "I don't know if I'm cut out for this secret agent stuff."

"What do you mean not cut out for it," said Scooter. "You were wonderful, chap! I'd still be on that island, laying in the sand while an angry turtle noshed on my leg."

"But Rontala," I replied. "I scared all of the islanders."

"Nonsense," said Glen. "They didn't even know that the princess was missing."

"They're right," said Millenia. "And you did find the passage way in the palace that showed how the culprit was able to nab the princess. Don't be so hard on yourself, Marc. You're doing a spectacular job."

I thought about it for a moment. Maybe they were right. I was new at this. I took a deep breath and looked at Millenia.

"What next?" I asked solidly.

"That's the spirit!" exclaimed the silhouette. "That's the determination that will help you succeed. That, my dear boy, is why you are part of the Order of the Cat."

I smiled.

"Well, then," I replied. "Let's get on with it."

"Where to next, fellas?" asked Scooter.

"You haven't yet been to see the doctor," said Glen. "What was his name?"

"Foulton," I responded. "Dr. Foulton."

Millenia said nothing, but I could hear him sigh.

"Yes," he said. "The doctor."

"Well," I said eagerly. "Should we go?"

"Yes," said Millenia hesitantly. "But be careful."

"I suggest you try a different approach," said Glen. "Just walking up to people and asking questions hasn't worked so far."

"I have an idea," said Scooter pulling his Loop from his jacket pocket. He dialed a number and spoke into the receiver. "Hello, King Letalia. This is Scooter. You don't happen to have Dr. Foulton's number do you? You do. Good. Yes. Okay," said Scooter. "Got it. Everything's great. Just working on a school project, that's all. Okay. Thanks. Goodbye."

"What are you doing?" I asked.

"You'll see," said Scooter as he dialed a new number into his Loop. He again put it up to his ear and spoke. "Hello, Dr. Foulton? Yes, this is Professor Blankenname from the Institute of Oceanic Studies. A pupil of mine and I are interested in touring your research vessel..."

Brilliant! Leave it to Scooter. He was, after all, a

genius.

"Oh, Marc," said Glen. "Before I forget. Your mother said to remind you that you need to meet with your tutor today at 2."

"Oh, man," I said. "I forgot. What'll I do?"

"Don't worry about it," said Glen. "This shouldn't take long. You'll be there and back before you know it."

Scooter hung up.

"Yes, Marc," said Scooter. "Don't worry about it. After all, you are going on a field trip with Professor Blankenname from the Institute for Oceanic Studies."

I laughed.

"Well, Professor Blankenname," I said. "Do we take a helicopter or a boat?"

"I feel like flying," said Scooter.

And he hit the panic button on the Loop.

Act 13:
THE GOOD DOCTOR...MAYBE

Scooter pretended to be a professor and arranged a tour of Dr. Foulton's research ship. We jumped into a helicopter and sped off to our meeting with Dr. Foulton.

"His research ship often anchors in the waters between Dontala and Rontala," said Scooter. "While on my yacht, I've passed by him there regularly."

"Do you think that he'll have any answers?" I asked.

"Doubtful," said Scooter. "But leave no stone unturned, eh Marcus."

I nodded. But for some reason I was more nervous this time. Something, I felt, was going to happen. Something big.

The helicopter flew out over the Pacific and when we were within eyesight of the two islands, I asked for the pilot to fly low. Soon we could see the research ship of Dr. Foulton, anchored right where Scooter remembered it to be.

"Slow down," I said. "We're going to jump."

"Jump!" exclaimed Scooter. "Are you mad?!"

"Glen gave me these Cons," I said. "It'll be all right."

"Oh yes," said Scooter calmly, suddenly remembering. "My loafers have the same treads."

He lifted his foot so that I could see the soles of his shoes. Sure enough: Converse.

The pilot swooped low over the boat and when we were nearby, it stopped, hovering in mid air. We both stood up on tip toes.

"Now!" I shouted.

Scooter and I jumped at the same time landing squarely and softly on the deck of the ship. The helicopter took off like a shot and we were left standing alone on Dr. Foulton's vessel.

Suddenly, a man in a white shirt and green trousers appeared from the stairs at the far end of the deck.

"What are you kids doing?!" he exclaimed. "I saw that. You could have been killed. Who are you? Why are you on my ship?"

I did not say a word. Scooter suddenly chimed in.

"Dr. Foulton," he said. "I'm Professor Blankenname from the Institute of Oceanic Studies. I'm here on a field trip with my pupil. Don't you remember? We arranged this earlier."

"That's right," I said. "We're here to learn about..."

I had no idea what to say.

"The ocean," chimed in Scooter. "We're here to learn about the ocean."

Dr. Foulton eyed both of us with suspicion.

"I do remember now," said Dr. Foulton. "But you're a little young to be a professor, aren't you?"

"The oceans hold new mysteries, Doctor. It's a young science" said Scooter. Then he proudly added, "And I'm a genius."

Leave it to Scooter to always mention that fact. The Doctor scratched his head and nodded.

"Yes," he said. "Yes. I think that I do recall that you were coming. Come inside," he said motioning with his hands. "We'll talk in there."

Something told me that we had made a mistake coming here. It was the same nagging feeling that I had in the helicopter. But there was nothing that could be done about it now. We had no choice but to stick to our story and find out what we could.

"Would you like some tea?" asked Dr. Foulton.

"Yes, sir," said Scooter cheerfully. "It's a little early in the day, but I'd love some."

"And you, what did you say your name was?" asked Foulton.

"Bob," I said without thinking.

"Bob," said Foulton. "Would you like some tea?"

"No thanks," I said. I followed as best as I could. "I'm allergic."

"Yes," said Foulton.

Just then, I noticed his eyes. They were a piercing green color, that became more frightening every time he squinted.

"Tea allergies are strange, aren't they," said Foulton to me.

"Huh," I responded, still caught in his steely gaze.

"Tea allergies," repeated the Doctor. "I said that they're strange."

"Yes," I said. "Strange indeed."

"How about a soda?" he asked.

"Sure," I said. "I'll take a Coke."

We sat at a small table in the ship's galley with our drinks and talked.

"So what do you want to learn about?" questioned Dr. Foulton.

"Well," said Scooter. "My institute has learned that you are testing a new way to purify seawater. I was curious if you could demonstrate for us."

"Certainly," said the doctor. "Finish your drinks and we'll have a display."

Scooter and I quickly downed the beverages. Then Dr. Foulton stood up and walked toward the door.

"This way, boys," he said motioning with his hand. "Follow me."

We both stood and followed the doctor to the door.

Walking out onto the deck, I began to feel dizzy. My vision was blurred. I looked at Scooter and saw three of him.

"Come over here," said the Doctor. "Come down these steps into the ship's hull and you'll see all that you need to see."

"I think that I need to sit down," said Scooter. "That was mighty strong tea, chap."

"Me too," I said. "I'm feeling dizzy."

I looked to Scooter again just in time to see him fall over.

"Oh, no," I said.

Everything around me began to spin.

"Did you put something in my drink?" I slurred.

A moment later, the lights went out and I was asleep.

Act 14:
THE DISCOVERY

I awakened to a dimly lit room. A small ray of light shone in through a porthole, and I could see Scooter lying on the floor next to me. I was still feeling a little drowsy, but I reached over and shook him.

"Scooter, wake-up."

Scooter rolled over and groaned.

"Oh, what happened?" he asked.

"I think that the doctor put something in our drinks," I said. "We must have passed-out."

"Where are we?" said Scooter, his voice weak. "Oh, my head. It hurts."

"You fell pretty hard," I said. "I think that we're in the hull of the doctor's ship."

"We've got to get out of here and find the princess," said Scooter.

"Then look no further," said a voice from out

of the darkness.

I looked around, but my eyes were still adjusting to the lack of light. As my vision cleared, I could see the outline of a small figure in the corner of the room.

"Who are you?" I demanded.

The figure moved towards us as Scooter slowly sat up. When the figure finally reached the patch of light from the window, Scooter let out an excited shout.

"Princess Telia!"

There stood a young girl who was my age. Her hair was done in thick black braids and held back from her face in a tail. She wore a green tank top with black cargo pants and boots. This was not the frilly princess that I expected when I saw her pink room.

Scooter jumped to his feet and ran to her.

"We've been looking for you," said Scooter.

"Scooter Brosnan," she said. "What are you doing here?"

"I, I," stammered Scooter. "I'm, ah, well..."

It was amazing. Scooter was at a loss for words. I immediately took over.

"We're here to rescue you," I said.

"Rescue me," she said. She stopped suddenly. "You're Marc John Jefferies."

"Yes," I replied.

"I've seen all of your movies," she said quickly. "Can I get an autograph?"

"Yes, but I'm afraid we don't have time for that now," I responded as respectfully as I could. "We've got to rescue you."

"Some rescue," she responded sarcastically. "Now you're both captured too."

"Some rescue!" I said. "That's nice. We come here to help you out and all you've got to say is 'some rescue.'"

"Well," she rebutted. "You two did get captured."

"Good point," I said. "But I don't see you escaping on your own." 'Take that princess,' I thought to myself.

"Well I don't see you stopping a war," she retorted.

She had another good point. This was one tough princess. And cute too. I flashed her a smile, and she turned away. That's what I thought – shy inside. She immediately changed the subject.

"What next?" she asked.

"Well," I said. "We hadn't thought of that yet."

"Did my father send you two looking for me?" she asked.

"No," I replied. "We came on our own."

"But how did you find me?" she wanted to know.

"Well," I argued. "We didn't know that you'd be here. Actually, it was an accident. You see, we found out that you were kidnapped..."

And then I told her the entire story. I began to explain about the Order of the Cat and our mission. I told her about my silly flying and the ferocious battle with the turtle. The princess listened intently as I told her everything that I was not supposed to tell.

"Boogieman," said Scooter. "You're giving away all of our secrets."

"Don't worry," said the princess. "I won't tell. Besides, who would ever believe that Scooter Brosnan was a secret agent."

"Well," said Scooter. "I, you know- ah..." he stammered on.

She laughed a little and Scooter blushed. I had seen him talk to kings and queens. I had seen him stand tall in the face of disaster and I had even gotten a pep talk from him when I doubted myself. But for all his smarts, and all his brilliance, Scooter could not talk to girls.

"How did you get here?" I asked her.

"I had just returned to my room," she began. "I opened my closet door to hang up my coat when suddenly everything inside spun around and revealed this man standing there! I screamed, but he put his hand over my mouth and told me to

81

follow him. He said that the castle was being invaded by Rontala and Dontala and that we must escape. When I tried to explain to him that I had just made peace with the tribes, he grabbed me, threw me over his shoulder, and ran down the secret passage way. Then he shouted 'flip flip' and the door to the secret tunnel closed. I couldn't fight him off, and I've been locked in this room ever since."

Scooter and I looked at one another.

"How did he know that the passage was there?" I asked.

"I have no idea, old bean," said Scooter. "I just don't know."

But before we could talk about it further, the door to the room burst open. Dr. Foulton appeared.

"Good," he said. "You've awakened just in time to meet your end."

I jumped to my feet.

"Who are you working for?" I said.

"I work for myself, you little runt," replied Foulton. "I work for me."

"You've kidnapped Princess Telia," I announced. "And we've caught you. Now give up."

Dr. Foulton laughed.

"You're right," he said. "I did kidnap the

princess, but I will not be giving up."

"But why," I asked. "Why kidnap the princess?"

"To start a war between Dontala and Rontala," said Dr. Foulton. "And to spread chaos to the world."

"You were planning on stealing the special plants," said Scooter.

The doctor laughed again.

"Stupid boys. There are no special plants," chuckled Dr. Foulton. "You've missed the boat on this one."

"Then why start a war?" demanded the princess.

"For power," he said. "Without the princess, King Letalia's kingdom would surely be dragged into the mess. And once everyone had destroyed each other, I would come back to take the throne."

"It would not have been that easy," said Scooter.

"Oh no," said Dr. Foulton. "I managed to get past the kingdom's defenses. I can do anything."

"How did you pass the guards?" asked Scooter.

"Flip, flip," said Dr. Foulton.

"How do you know about that password?" I demanded.

"Who do you think built the palace?" said

Dr. Foulton. "That's right – the Order of the Cat."

"But how do you know about the Order of The Cat?" I said.

Dr. Foulton reached into his shirt pocket and pulled out a pin, just like the one that I carried; just like the one that Scooter and Glen carried. On the pin was a claw and a cattail: the sign of the Order of the Cat!

"Because I, too, was once a member of the Order of the Cat," he said. "From the moment you kids landed on my ship, I knew who you were working for."

"But you couldn't be. Our job is justice," said Scooter. "We're supposed to be the good guy."

"I was the good guy," said the Doctor. "But I wanted more. I deserved more."

"You're greedy," exclaimed the princess. "You wouldn't have used the throne to help people as my family has done. You would have used if for your own selfish purpose."

"That's good enough for me," said Dr. Foulton. "And now, kids, the end is here."

Scooter jumped to his feet.

"Not if I can help it!" he shouted.

Scooter reached his hand into his coat pocket to grab something. Suddenly his eyes became wide.

"Looking for this?" asked Dr. Foulton.

Foulton held something small in his hand. It was the Loop!

"Oh no," said Scooter. "I must have dropped it when we jumped."

"And now it's mine," said the doctor. "Finders keepers. Goodbye brats!"

He slammed the door shut and locked it from the other side. Scooter and I raced over to open it but could not. We tugged and tugged but nothing happened. I threw myself against the door, but it would not budge. And then, suddenly we heard a great explosion.

BOOM!

The entire ship lurched.

"What's happening!" shouted the princess.

Scooter and I ran to the window, but neither of us could see out. It was too high up.

"Here," said Scooter making a step with his hands. "Climb up."

Scooter quickly boosted me up onto his shoulders, and I looked out of the porthole. The doctor was racing away in a speed boat. I looked toward the front of the ship. It was gone! He had blown it up, and we were now sinking rapidly. I could see the water rising.

"Scooter," I said. "The ship is sinking!"

We ran around the room looking for another way out, but there was none. I looked up to the porthole. Water was rising all around us. Suddenly the ship rolled on its side sending us flying across the room. The room got darker and darker, and I realized that we were under water.

"The port hole," said the princess. "It's our only hope."

Scooter ran over to a heavy brass bell that had fallen off of a table.

"Marc," he said. "Help me with this. We'll use it to break the window."

I ran to him. We picked-up the bell, and with all of our might, tossed it and sent it crashing through the port hole, shattering the glass. Water poured in, and the cabin began to flood.

"Now what?" begged the princess.

"The Bubble Sticks," I said. I pulled mine from my pocket, and Scooter did the same. "Here princess," I said handing her the Bubble Stick. "You can use this to breathe under water."

"What about you?" she asked.

"I can hold my breath longer than any fish," I said. "There's no time. Do it!"

The princess and Scooter put the straws in their mouths and scuttled out of the port hole and into the ocean. Scooter had lost his Loop, but I still had my own. I hit the panic button on that thing, took a last giant gulp of air, and dove in after them.

The water was warm as I swam toward the surface, the ship falling into the ocean depths behind me. The light got brighter and brighter, and suddenly, I burst through the top of the water, gasping for air. Scooter and the princess were already floating alongside of me.

"We did it!" shouted Scooter. "Jolly fine work, my friend."

He threw out his hand for a high five, and we hit. Just then, the helicopter appeared on the horizon as promised.

"What's that?" asked the princess.

"That's our ride, your highness," I said.

The cable lowered down to us. After we made certain that the princess was safely loaded, Scooter and I latched on and climbed aboard. Unfortunately, Foulton had vanished.

Act 15:
ANSWERS

We raced back to the movie set. We had the princess with us, and it seemed that our mission was accomplished. But I had questions.

We arrived back on the set and went looking for Glen. We burst into his trailer. He was seated on the floor in the middle of his mess eating an avocado and Spam sandwich. The POKEY sat next to him.

"Princess Telia?" asked Glen, his mouth full of food.

"Yes," she replied. "What is that you're eating?"

"Avocado and Spam," said Glen. "On rye."

She winced.

"Would you like a bite?" Glen asked holding the sandwich out to her.

"No thank you," she said politely.

just then, Glen's eyes lit up.

"Scooter, what are you doing here?" asked Glen.

"What do you mean, chap?" replied Scooter. "Where would I be?"

Glen pointed down to the POKEY.

"I'm tracking your Loop, and it appears that you're moving across the ocean at an outrageous speed," said Glen.

"My Loop!" Scooter responded. "It seems that dropping it was a stroke of luck."

I turned my attention to Glen.

"Glen, I need to speak with Millenia," I said. "Now."

"Okay," said Glen puzzled. "Is everything alright?"

"I don't know," I responded. "That's why I need to talk to Millenia."

"You got it," said Glen. "Scooter, grab the shades."

Scooter ran around the room and pulled all of the blinds closed.

Clap! Clap!

Glen banged his hands together and the lights went out.

"My sandwich!" came Glen's voice from the dark. "What a mess. Oh well."

And then the familiar shadow appeared on the wall.

"Greetings," said Millenia. "Princess Telia, I presume."

"Yes," said the princess. "And you must be Millenia."

"Yes," said Millenia. "I see that someone has been sharing some secrets."

"Yes," I said. "But some of us have not."

"Marc," said Millenia. "What is it?"

"Dr. Foulton," I began. "He had a pin. He had a pin just like ours from the Order of the Cat. And he knew everything about us. How?"

"Tell me, Marc," said Millenia. "Did this man have green eyes?"

"Yes," I said assuredly.

"Eyes that pierced through you when he stared?" said Millenia.

"Evil eyes," I said.

Millenia paused and then sighed.

"I suspected this, but had no idea that it was possible until now," said the old shadow.

"What?" I demanded.

"His name was once Bartholomew Foulton," said Millenia. "But the other members called him by his code name, Bad Bart, because he had a knack for creating mischief. He hated the name though. One day, he simply disappeared, never to be heard from again. At least, not until now. Rather than come to us and tell us what was wrong, he ran away without thinking first."

"So he was a member of the Order of the Cat?"

asked Scooter.

"I don't understand," I said. "What happened to make Dr. Foulton turn bad?"

Millenia sighed.

"I do not know," he said. "He was once a promising student of mine, very much interested in science, especially chemistry."

"Your student," said Scooter inquisitively.

"Yes," said Millenia. "We lost track of him some time ago, and it was not until he revealed his identity to you Marc, that we were able to piece it all together. The last time that we saw him, he was only a boy."

"You should have told us," I said. "We should have known. We walked in there unprepared."

"You are right, Marc John Jefferies," said Millenia. "And for my mistake, I am sorry. I did not know."

I stared at the figure on the screen, and although I could not see his face, his voice meant every word of what he just said. I took a deep breath and spoke.

"Apology accepted," I said. "Now. What next?"

"We're still tracking Foulton on the POKEY," said Glen.

"Glen," I said. "Can you download the coordinates of Scooter's Loop into mine?"

"Sure," said Glen. "Why?"

"The mission's not over," I responded.

"Marc," said Millenia. "You've got the princess.

You don't have to go after him."

"I know," I said. "But he has something of ours that I want."

"Understood," said Millenia. "May victory smile upon you, Marc John Jefferies."

"Thank you," I said, and the shadow disappeared.

"It's been a heck of a couple of days for you," said Scooter.

"It's not over yet," I responded. "But it's not over yet."

"Well," said the princess. "What are we waiting for?"

I turned toward her. She had a big grin on her face. I pulled the Loop from my pocket and hit the panic button.

And we were off again.

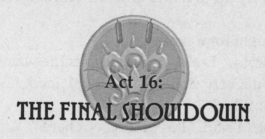

Act 16:
THE FINAL SHOWDOWN

Using my Loop, we tracked the evil Dr. Foulton to a tiny desert island. Unlike the rest of the sandy beaches that I had seen in this part of the world, the shoreline on this one was covered with rocks. We were hovering very low and far away from the place, so the pilot handed me a pair of binoculars so that I could see better.

In the middle of the island was a large cement building. It was plain on the outside, and except for a few fancy looking windows, it had no decoration. I described it to the princess.

"What is that place?" I asked.

She took the binoculars from me. She shrugged her shoulders.

"I don't know," she confessed. "We're not that far from my island, but I've never seen this place before."

"Well that's where he is," I said. "And that's where we need to go."

"How will we get in, pal?" asked Scooter. "We can't just fly up to it and land on the roof. He'll spot us."

I thought for a moment.

"Princess," I said. "How deep is the water here?"

"Oh, it's very shallow," she explained. "Always has been. Why?"

"Pilot," I said. "I'm getting out here."

"What!?" exclaimed Scooter. "Boyo, are you mad?"

"No, not mad," I said. "But he's got something that belongs to us, and I want it back."

"The Loop?" asked Scooter.

"The pin," I responded. "A man like him doesn't deserve to wear it."

"Maybe we should wait for reinforcements," said Scooter. "Besides, chap, I'm still a little dizzy."

"There's no time," I replied. "You stay with the princess, Scooter. I'm going after the doctor. Princess, may I have that Bubble Stick back?"

She pulled the special straw from her pocket and handed it to me.

"Pilot, take us lower," I instructed.

"Good luck, Marc," said the princess.

The helicopter dipped down toward the water. I once more secured the Loop in my cargo pocket, turned to my new friends, gave them a wink, and with a light jump (no tip toes for this one,) I hopped into the water.

I hit the ocean with a small PLUNK! Soon I was sinking down, down, down to the bottom. I put the Bubble Stick in my mouth, and just as Glen had promised, I could breathe under water.

About fifteen feet below the surface, I touched down. The ocean floor was as rocky as the shoreline, and once I got the hang of the currents, walking down below was easy. Within a few minutes, I had reached the rugged beach.

I climbed cautiously from the water, and staying on my belly, slid across the rocks towards the cement structure. No sounds could be heard, and there was no sign of the doctor.

I reached the building, quickly stood, and threw my back against the wall. Moving slowly along its edge, I made my way down the side and around the corner. There I caught sight of the doctor's speedboat tied hastily to an old wooden dock. A door was immediately to my left, and peaking cautiously around the corner, I attempted to look inside. A long corridor stretched deep into the complex. I took a deep breath, and with all of my courage went inside.

The hall was covered in mildew and musty smelling like an old cellar. Rotting fishing nets hung from the walls with cobwebs stretched between them. My footsteps echoed through the silence, so I began to walk softer and slower, being careful not to give myself away.

I rounded another corner and still another, going deeper and deeper into the maze. This went on for some time, and just when I thought that there couldn't possibly be another room, I came to a dead end. A small shadow moved across my path, and beyond it, a dim light shone out from a room in the distance. With catlike stealth, I moved to the entrance of that room. Again with my back to the wall, I slowly peered around the corner.

The room was overflowing with electronics. Computers filled every nook and cranny, and in the middle, at a work table, was my target: Dr. Foulton.

I stepped around the corner, took one last deep breath, and puffed up my chest to look bigger than I really was. Yes, I was the perfect secret agent, but I was still only the size of a thirteen year old. Oh well. Now or never. I spoke.

"The game is up, Foulton," I said.

He spun around.

"Bob," he exclaimed. "How did you escape?!"

"It's Boogieman to you," I responded. "I believe that you have something that belongs to me."

He smiled and then laughed. He reached into his pocket and pulled out Scooter's Loop.

"Is this what you want," said Dr. Foulton shaking

it in his hand. "Sorry, Boogieman, but I don't think so."

With a burst of energy he threw the Loop onto the floor, shattering it sending a million pieces of broken plastic everywhere.

"Now what are you going to do," he chuckled.

"That's not what I came for," I said. "Your pin. Give it to me."

"Why should I?" he asked. "Why should I do what you say?"

"Because you are no longer part of the Order of the Cat," I responded. "We only do good."

"Silly boy," he called. "Is that all? Well then, here. Never cared for it much anyway."

He took the pin out of his pocket, set it on the table, and stepped away from it.

"You, young man, may have it."

He took another step away from the table and stared at me. I wasn't sure what to make of this, but there the pin was, sitting just a few feet away. I walked slowly towards the table, and Dr. Foulton took another step back. I stopped in my tracks.

"Go ahead, boy," he taunted. "Take it. If you can."

We locked eyes for a moment, staring intently at one another. I looked at the pin, looked at Dr. Foulton, and then back to the pin again. I was still a long way away from the table. Slowly, I stood on tiptoes.

"Go on," he chuckled again. "Take it. I dare you."

"Okay," I said.

And with that, I sprang from my position, crossing the room in one leap and snatching the pin from the table. The doctor's eyes opened wide. He ran to one corner of the room.

"So you have what you came for," he said. "Now see what you can do with this."

He lunged over to a computer, tapped one of the keys, and the door that I had come in slammed shut behind me.

"I missed a chance to get rid of you once. I won't do it twice. So long, Bob!"

And he ran out of an exit at the other end of the room, that door slamming down behind him as well. An alarm sounded and an electronic sounding voice came over the loudspeaker.

"Self destruct activated. This building will self destruct in ten seconds. Nine seconds. Eight seconds..."

I ran toward the exit and tugged at the metal door, but it would not move.

"Not again!" I exclaimed.

"Seven seconds," said the electronic voice. "Six seconds..."

I had to act quickly or else this was the end. Both doors locked and not a window in this room. What to do!

"Five, seconds. Four seconds..."

And then an idea hit me.

"FLIP, FLIP!" I shouted. "FLIP, FLIP!"

Computers swung around. Tables turned over and over. The lights hanging in the middle of the room pulled up through the ceiling and came back down again.

I ran toward the nearest secret passage. It was a crate that kept moving back and forth in front of the wall.

"Three seconds. Two seconds..."

"FLIP, FLIP!" I shouted one last time at the top of my lungs. The crate slid aside, and I dove into the hole that appeared there.

"FLIP, FLIP!" I screamed and water poured into the hole. Suddenly the crate slid closed behind me, the bottom dropped out from under me, and I was in the dark, sliding down a dark tunnel, water pouring over me, twisting and turning every which way. Still sliding, spiraling downward, faster and faster in the dark, until...

WHOOSH!

I flew out of the side of the building and skidded across the top of the water.

SPLOOSH! as I hit the ocean.

"One," said the electronic voice from an outside speaker. I turned my head just in time to see the entire building fall down.

CRASH! A big ball of dust went into the air.

"I MADE IT!" I shouted.

The helicopter swooped in nearby, and I lifted my arm up out of the water to signal it. The hook lowered down to me. I grabbed on, and still dripping like a newly caught mackerel, I was hoisted once again to safety. Turning around...

"Boogieman!" exclaimed Scooter.

He threw his hand into the air and we high fived.

"That was awesome," said the princess.

She leaned in toward me, and gently kissed my cheek. I could feel my face redden.

"Are you okay?" she asked.

I nodded yes.

"How do you feel, chap?" asked Scooter.

I reached up and felt my soaking hair. Water dripped off of my nose."Wet," was all that I could manage.

They laughed, and with that, we made our way home.

Act 17:
REPORT TO MILLENIA

We were all soon safely back where we belonged. The princess went home to her grateful father, and Scooter and I joined Glen in his trailer to explain to Millenia what had happened. The POKEY projected the mysterious silhouette once more onto Glen's window shade.

"Not bad work, Marc John Jefferies," said Millenia.

"But Dr. Foulton still got away," I said.

"Yes he did," said Millenia. "But you saved the princess and helped to keep peace amongst the tribes, and that is what counts. For that, I am thankful."

I smiled. Saving the world felt good.

"Here," I said, holding the pin up so that everyone could see. "This is Foulton's. I got it back."

"Impressive, Marc. Most impressive," said

Millenia. "You've protected the integrity of our order."

I would gladly take the complements all day.

"It's dangerous work," continued Millenia. "Always think first. Some things you can't take back once they are done. Understand."

"Yes," I said sheepishly, nodding my head.

"And that is a lesson that you have taught me," continued Millenia.

"The lesson I taught you?" I said.

"Yes, Marc," said Millenia. "And I thank you."

"But what about Bad Bart," said Scooter. "Can't let a bugger like that off so easily."

"Don't worry about the good doctor," said Millenia. "His time will come. For now, victory has once again smiled upon the Order of the Cat."

Glen jumped out of his seat.

"This calls for a celebration!" he exclaimed. "Spam and avocados anyone?"

We all groaned.

"Thank you, but no," said Millenia. "And with that I leave you."

The POKEY went dark, and Millenia disappeared.

"Now what?" I asked.

"We've got a movie to finish," said Glen.

The three of us left Glen's trailer, and just as we were walking out the door, my parents appeared from out of nowhere.

"Marc John Jefferies," said my father. "Where have you been?"

"You missed your tutoring session," said my mother. "Did Glen give you the watch."

"Oh, man," I groaned.

I turned toward Glen as he mouthed the words 'I forgot. Sorry.'

"Well," said my father. "Let's hear it."

"Excuse me," said Scooter. "Allow me to introduce myself. I am Scooter Brosnan of the Westport, Connecticut Brosnans."

"Who are you?" asked my mother.

"Why, Mrs. Jefferies," said Scooter. "Didn't they tell you. I'm Marc's new tutor."

He threw his arms around each of my parent's shoulders and began to walk with them.

"Where have you been all day?" questioned my father.

"On a field trip," said Scooter. "On a field trip studying the ocean."

He glanced over his shoulder at me and winked. Good old Scooter.

"Let me tell you all about it." And he led them away.

So, now you know. You know that I am a secret agent who has saved the world. I have met a king and found a princess. I have swam out of a sinking ship, and saved my friends from danger, and even managed to finish a movie while I was doing it. But I've got to say, if you think all that's rough...

Try algebra.

Till next time...

-MJJ, The Real Deal

Marc John Jefferies' Director's Sheet

A.

Abode – a place where someone lives or stays

Anarchy – a society without government where things are out of control

B.

Befitting – something that is proper, right, or suitable

Bestow – to give something as a gift

Brilliant – shinning brightly or sparkling

C.

Cavernous – a very large place full of caverns or caves

Chandelier – a lighting fixture hanging from the ceiling

Chaos – great disorder where everything is out of control

D.

Dejected – when someone is not feeling well or is in low spirits because they are not accepted

Devastate – to destroy something

Distraught – very sad and nervous at the same time

E.
Eccentric – someone who does not act normally and displays strange behavior as part of his or her regular personality

Exotic – something rare and at times beautiful

Extraordinary – when something is out of the ordinary or is exceptional

F.
Flourish – to blossom or grow

G.
Galley – the kitchen area of a boat

H.
Hull – the main body of a boat where people and supplies are kept

L.
Lurch – to suddenly move quickly to one side or the other

M.
Marvelous – something that is surprising and wonderful at the same time

Moored – something held with a cable or rope, typically a boat

P.
Prosperous – having continual success at something

S.
Scrolls – ancient forms of books that were rolled into long circular storage cases

Silhouette – any dark shape seen against a dark background

Sinister – the act of being evil or bad

Summoned – to be called toward something

Suspicious – to be careful and curious at the same time

T.
Trek – a rough and labored walk like a hike

Marc John Jefferies' Gyroscope

Alexandria – Built by Alexander the Great in 337 BC, Alexandria was the second largest city in the ancient world with a population of over 2.5 million people! The library established in Alexandria was the largest ever designed in the history of the world and drew students from all over who wanted to study the books it housed.

Ancient Egypt – Egypt was a magnificent seaside country of the ancient world known for its advanced culture and beautiful architectural marvels. Egypt was the home of the pyramids which are believed to be one of the seven wonders of the ancient world. It was a place where many of the world's most intelligent people lived so that they could study at the great Library of Alexandria. Did you know that Egypt is three times the size of the State of New Mexico?

Cleopatra – Cleopatra was the last of a long line of great Kings and Queens in ancient Egypt. She was the most powerful woman in the history of the ancient world and known by everyone for her amazing beauty. Many of her subjects believed that she was a god.

Pacific Ocean – The Pacific Ocean is the largest body of water on the face of the planet. If it were not so salty it could provide everyone in the world with enough water to last billions of years.

River Nile – The Nile is a great river that runs through Egypt. It was worshiped by ancient people because they believed it had special healing powers.

Romans – Rome was once a nation of its own but now is a city that is located in the modern European country of Italy. It has a colorful and exciting history. The ancient gladiators played their games there in the coliseum which was the earliest form of our modern football stadium. The Romans were a powerful people who were respected everywhere in the ancient world.

Fighting alongside his quirky sidekick, Scooter Brosnan, Marc embarks on a series of adventures that carry him to multiple countries to face multiple foes. On the trail, he finds his way into and out of trouble, greets mystery and intrigue with a joke and a smile, and even bumps into a little romance - all while acting for the camera and finishing his homework!

The Secret Agent MJJ series is a thrill ride through life's lessons and adventures and has a universal appeal that is sure to delight boys and girls of all ages. Discover and learn with Marc John Jefferies in a way that only MJJ, The Real Deal, can provide.

Need more adventure and excitement?

Visit **www.marcjohnonline.com** to find information on a Marc John Jefferies Adventure Party coming to a city near you. And be sure to look for these spectacular new titles on the website or the shelves of your local bookstore.

#2: The Secret Portrait
Follow Marc as he winds his way through the dark and abandoned train tunnels beneath Yankee Stadium in pursuit of a stolen painting that will save the world from certain doom. Join Marc and his hero, baseball legend Ron Gatling, as they track down the secret portrait.

#3: The Volcano
Marc meets up with new friends and companions as they travel into the center of a rumbling volcano. Will they keep the mountain from erupting or will The Order of the Snake prevail in its quest for world domination and chaos? Follow Marc as he throws himself into harms way to stop a disaster that is anything but natural.

Wait! There's more!
Coming soon...

#4: The Fountain of Youth   #6: The Sun King
#5: The Pirates of Marathon   #7: The Mad Conductor

Go see Marc's movies!

www.marcjohnonline.com

Marc on the small screen...

This is Roy, the character Marc John Jefferies plays on Mr. Bill Cosby's new animated show, "Fatherhood." See it on Nickelodeon.